Author's Note:

This story is loosely based on Ganesh and Karthikeya's (Karthik for short) race around the world, which is a popular tale in Hinduism. In the original telling, Karthik and Ganesh race around the world to win the world's tastiest mango. While Karthik attempted to use his muscular physique to conquer the challenge, Ganesh used his brains. He walked around his parents stating that they were his world, and was awarded the prize for this touching act and his wisdom. In fact, to this day, Hindu families around the world think of Ganesh when they embark on a challenging endeavor. They look to Ganesh to remove obstacles and grace them with his wisdom.

This book is not a retelling of the popular Hindu tale. Many details have been altered in this adaptation. In an attempt to make the adaptation more relatable for children, themes of bullying and friendship have been highlighted.

Thank you for helping rebuild Nepal after the devastating 4/25/15 earthquake.
A portion of our proceeds from the first run of *Ganesh & the Little Mouse*
will go directly towards Nepalese earthquake relief.

Ojovati Joshi · Vyas Joshi · Naresh & Sushma Manaktola · Neal Manaktola · Prakash Desai · Namrata Deshmukh · Mira & Kirin · Kathleen O'mara · Andrea Macrae · Erin Davis · Jeanie Para · Adrienne Bruno · Rachna Butani · Amy Patel · Nitya Rai · Saia Patel · Unjali Malhotra · Veena Sharma · Teia Patel · Katherine Perry · Nina Moe · Deepti Shenoy · Baby Yoganathan 2015 · Vani Ku · The Libon Family · Vaishnavi Sannidhanam · Charulata Joshi · Finley Neu · Max Wylie · Rujuta Limaye · Sweta Gowda · Shena Wolf · Anna Bernhardt · Sheetal Shah · Katelyn Shore · Flory & Perrie Bouldin · William Behram Mintz · Dhilan Rao · Chelsea Condos · Cindy Nowak · Sayali & Suhas Marathe · Ashley Collette · Sinthiya Siva · Baby Stelk · Senthuran Pooranananthan · Yavanan Bertram · Matthew Weiser · Sulagna Bharati · Leslie Burkland · Valerie Grabiel · Vishwas Pethe · Shreya Deb · Riya Vipoositha Gnanenthra · Mila Harmandarian · Sonal Uban · Mohita Mohan · Tehsin Bhayani · Kunal Preeti · Kobeeka Sundaranathan · Jeshmin Bhaju · Edgardo Marinkovic · Shreyas, Pradipta, & Saranga Komanduri · Laura Grimaldo · Andrea Brereton · Rajeeve Ganeshalingam · Sharschchandra Bidargaddi · Mital Chheda · Rahul Arora · Rita Jain · Urmila (Aji) Joshi · Keyur Tripathi · Ishan & Saavan Chima · Rita Sharma · Puja Shetty · Stephanie Chang · Rohini Joshi · Megha Parikh · Dylan Jay Patel · Caroline & Eleanor Kaplan · Laura Palma · Amelia Susan Lester · Neera Bahri · Laura Taylor · Raje Shwari · James R. Williams · Neelam Patel · Jaya Doobay · Tarun Babbar · Sachin Rustagi · Angelica Fematt-Davidson · Jean Gibson · Nitesh Kumar · Smita Gholkar · C Roxanne Karayil · Hashika · Latha Menon · Deepti Murali · Emma Hollander · Suneel Sundar · Aarti Goel · Amit Kulshrestha · Krishna & Shiva Suri · Yumi Yasutake · Neha Parikh · Gordon Marx · Anita Nobile · Avni Patel · Jasper Schlubach

To Ammama. Thanks for all the undralu.
Love, Saila & Sri

For my son, Aashay: run far & climb high, & know
that I will always love & support you.
Anjali Joshi

For Duncan and Maggie, who are my world.
-CSM

GANESH AND THE LITTLE MOUSE

www.mascotbooks.com | www.bharatbabies.com

Ganesh and the Little Mouse

For more information, please contact:
Mascot Books | 560 Herndon Parkway #120 | Herndon, VA 20170
info@mascotbooks.com

Library of Congress Control Number: 2015911877

CPSIA Code: PRT0915A
ISBN-13: 978-1-63177-299-3

Printed in the United States

High in the sky, beyond the moon and above the clouds, there is a grand kingdom.
The kingdom is filled with beautiful, powerful gods and goddesses who reign the world below.

Lord Shiva, Goddess Parvati, and their two sons Ganesh and Karthik lived in this grand kingdom. They were a happy family. Like all the other gods in the kingdom, Ganesh and Karthik were both powerful and intelligent. Their parents were very proud of them.

Although they loved and cared for him, Ganesh was different from the rest of his family. He had the head of an elephant. Ganesh also had an unusual best friend – a little mouse.

Ganesh and Little Mouse ate together, played together, and even traveled together with Ganesh riding on Little Mouse's back.

Some of the gods would tease Ganesh about his little friend. "Look at that tiny mouse Ganesh is riding on!" they would laugh. Even Ganesh's brother Karthik would chime in. Karthik would sit by his beloved peacock, stroking her blue tail. "Blue Peacock is quick, graceful, and beautiful. What can your Little Mouse do?"

Fists clenched and holding back tears, Ganesh yelled back, "Little Mouse is the bravest, smartest, and most loving creature in this kingdom!"

Ganesh's mother comforted him. Her warmth gave Ganesh the courage to hold his head up high.

Ganesh's father sat him down and explained that not everyone understood the depth of his friendship with Little Mouse. Ganesh listened to his father's words; they gave him the strength to pay no attention to the laughter and mocking words of others.

One day, while out for a walk, Ganesh saw a sign.

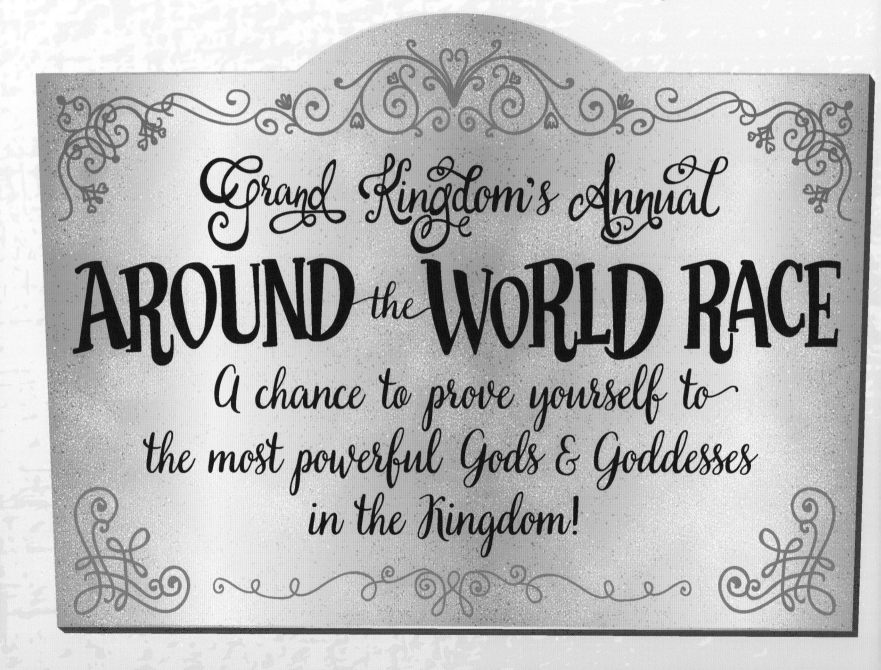

Grand Kingdom's Annual

AROUND the WORLD RACE

A chance to prove yourself to the most powerful Gods & Goddesses in the Kingdom!

Ganesh had a wonderful idea! He ran to the garden to find Little Mouse and show him the sign. "Will you participate in this year's race with me?" he asked Little Mouse eagerly. Little Mouse was hesitant. He was worried he would disappoint his friend. But he could see how much the race meant to Ganesh, so he agreed.

Grand Kingdom's Annual
AROUND the WORLD RACE
A chance to prove yourself to the most powerful Gods & Goddesses in the Kingdom!

The next day, Ganesh announced to all the gods and goddesses in the kingdom that he and Little Mouse would be entering the race. Surya, the Sun God, was the first to laugh. "Oh, Ganesh, you think your Little Mouse can beat my chariot of seven horses?" he chortled. "My horses are the fastest and most powerful racers in the world!"

Chandra, the Moon God, joined in. "Ganesh, Ganesh, Ganesh! My antelope is quicker than you know. He can outrun the fastest of land animals. Your Little Mouse doesn't stand a chance!"

Sadly, even Ganesh's brother Karthik laughed at him. "You've lost your mind, brother! You're done for! Surya's horses, Chandra's antelope, and my peacock will leave you and your Little Mouse eating dust!"

But Ganesh remembered what his father and mother said, and he paid no attention to their words.

That night, Ganesh's mother spoke with him about the race. "Ganesh, why are you doing this?" she questioned quietly. "You don't need to prove yourself to anyone. Little Mouse is a true friend. That is what is truly important."

"I am tired of hearing their mocking words, Mother," Ganesh replied. "Little Mouse is fast, strong, and fierce like all the other animals. I want to show the world just how amazing Little Mouse is!" Ganesh's mother shook her head, but said no more.

Finally, the day of the big race came. Everyone in the kingdom came to watch Ganesh and his Little Mouse take on the world's fastest and most powerful competitors. When he looked into the crowd, he saw his mother's warm smile and his father's reassuring nod.

The judge stood along the sidelines, reviewing the rules. "Each participant and their animal must run around the world. The first to return will be the winner."

Ganesh and Little Mouse took their places alongside the other animals. Ganesh's heart was pounding. "Take your places, challengers," said the judge. "On your marks, get set, GO!" At once, Surya's chariot of horses leapt into action. Surya grasped tightly to the reins as they sped past the others.

Chandra's antelope darted behind, determined to steal the lead. Karthik's peacock moved quickly, her long tail bobbing behind her.

Ganesh and Little Mouse scurried behind the rest.
Within minutes, the horses, antelope, and peacock were miles
ahead and no longer in sight. Gasping for air, Little Mouse
began to slow down until finally he collapsed to the ground.

"Little Mouse! Little Mouse!"

Ganesh's mother screamed as she fought through the crowds and into the arena.
But the guards would not let her pass.

Little Mouse looked up at Ganesh with tears streaming down his little face. "My dear friend, I have failed you. I can't compete with the others. I can't sprint like a horse, dart like an antelope, or move quickly like a peacock. I am just a Little Mouse."

Ganesh shook his head. "No, you haven't failed me. I have failed you. How silly of me to suggest that we compete in a race around the world. I don't care if you are fast or powerful. You are my very best friend, and you are always there for me. You are my world."

At once, Ganesh knew
what he had to do.

He carefully picked up Little Mouse and made his way into the crowd where his mother and father stood. He placed his friend in his mother's hands and slowly walked around his parents and beloved friend.

He took a deep breath mustering all the courage he could summon. "I have completed the challenge. I have circled the world."

"Without my mother and father, I would not have courage or strength. Without Little Mouse, I would not have a true friend. They are my everything. They are my world."

Astonished by Ganesh's wisdom, and touched by his love towards his parents and Little Mouse, the entire kingdom rose to their feet. Applause roared throughout the arena. Even Surya, Chandra, and Karthik saw the undeniable truth in Ganesh's words. The entire kingdom unanimously agreed that Ganesh and Little Mouse were the winners of the race.

From that day forward, no one teased
Ganesh and Little Mouse about their unusual friendship.

About the Author: Anjali Joshi

Anjali has loved reading for as long as she can remember. Between the covers of books, she has gotten lost in magical worlds, befriended fictional characters, and been a part of epic journeys. As an educator, writer, and mother, Anjali's goal is to foster the love of reading and learning in the next generation. She is passionate about bringing diversity to children's literature and sharing stories of India's rich culture with our littlest adventurers.

About the Illustrator: Christy McCreery

Christy's love of art and illustration began in a library. From a young age, she was inspired by picture books and garnered hours of drawing practice by copying their illustrations. In grade school, she had Bill Peet's autobiography perpetually checked out and her dream was to become a Disney animator (or a marine biologist). These days, she spends most of her professional time in the world of advertising, but still gets most excited when a project provides her with the opportunity to draw. Christy has a BA in Studio Art from Wheaton College and Certificate of Art Direction from the Creative Circus in Atlanta, Georgia, where she lives with her husband and daughter.